MISS TRIMBLE'S TRAPDOOR

The Perseverance of Christopher Columbus

Lori Jordan-Rice

Illustrations by Fox Carlton Hughes

Synergy Books

Miss Trimble's Trapdoor: The Perseverance of Christopher Columbus
Published by Synergy Books
P.O. Box 80107
Austin, Texas 78758

For more information about our books, please write to us, call 512.478.2028, or visit
our website at www.synergybooks.net.

Copyright© 2009 by Lori Jordan-Rice
Illustrations by Fox Carlton Hughes

Publisher's Cataloging-in-Publication
(Provided by Quality Books, Inc.)

Jordan-Rice, Lori.
    Miss Trimble's trapdoor. The perseverance of
Christopher Columbus / Lori Jordan-Rice ; illustrated by
Fox Carlton Hughes.
        p. cm.
    SUMMARY: Eleven-year-old Tyler hated school until he
discovered a magical trapdoor beneath his desk, a
basement filled with old books, and a wise, talking dog.
Tyler travels into the past, sets sail aboard the Santa
Maria with Christopher Columbus and learns what
determination means.
    Audience: Ages 9-12.
    LCCN 2008910595
    ISBN-13: 978-0-9821601-5-2
    ISBN-10: 0-9821601-5-1

    1. Columbus, Christopher--Juvenile fiction.
2. Perseverance (Ethics)--Juvenile fiction. 3. Time travel
--Juvenile fiction. 4. America--Discovery and
exploration--Spanish--Juvenile fiction. [1. Columbus,
Christopher--Fiction. 2. Explorers--Fiction.
3. Perseverance (Ethics)--Fiction. 3. Time travel--
Fiction. 4. America--Discovery and exploration--Spanish
--Fiction.] I. Hughes, Fox Carlton, 1929- ill.
II. Title. III. Title: Perseverance of Christopher Columbus.

PZ7.J76814Misp 2009   [Fic]
              QBI08-600335

While this book is based on historical events and people, some situations and characters
are fictional and products of the author's imagination.

10 9 8 7 6 5 4 3 2 1

To Jarrett, Rylan, and Sterling

"Trying to plan for the future without a sense of the past is like trying to plant cut flowers."
—*Historian Daniel Boorstin*

TABLE OF CONTENTS

Note to Parents and Teachers

Basic U.S. history should be common knowledge, but it is not. Many educators and parents are concerned that our students are historically illiterate. They are taught history in school, but it doesn't seem to stick. Kids deem it boring or of little use.

My vision for the Miss Trimble's Trapdoor book series is to fill this need in a way that will delight children, teachers, and parents alike. The first book introduced Tyler, a struggling student who accidentally discovers a trapdoor beneath his desk that leads to a magical room in which he can visit any time in history. Readers joined Tyler as he took several brief visits back in time and learned the value of understanding history.

Each subsequent book in the series focuses on a single U.S. history concept in much greater detail while also teaching a moral lesson. In this second book, Tyler experiences firsthand what sailing on Christopher Columbus's ship is like. He learns not only the historical background of the great explorer, but also how the virtue of perseverance is important in his own life.

As Pulitzer Prize-winning historian David McCullough puts it, "Amnesia is as detrimental to society as to an individual." My goal is to lead children to an understanding of their national heritage in a way that will engage their enthusiasm. Join Tyler, his classmates, and his teacher as we remember our history!

Psssst...Hey, kids,

I don't know which one is worse, having to do an oral report in front of the whole class or trying out for the basketball team! I'm stuck doing both in the same month in Miss Trimble's class. I think I would rather have nothing to eat but broccoli for a whole month, but nobody asked my opinion. I guess I'm lucky that a few kids are being pretty cool to me about the whole thing. I'm also getting some help from my teacher and Mr. Jenkins, the custodian. Most of my help is coming from the stray dog that hangs around the school, Barnabas Bailey. I know it sounds crazy, but it's true. Keep reading to find out how he's teaching me about Christopher Columbus and that I should never give up!

Your friend,
Tyler Thompson

CHAPTER ONE

DREADED ANNOUNCEMENTS

The October morning air felt different as Tyler walked to school. He almost felt chilly in his short sleeves at such an early hour. Finally the warm, muggy September days were surrendering to the inevitable briskness of fall. The crisp, colorful leaves crunched beneath Tyler's feet as he sauntered along.

The pounding of a basketball against the playground pavement and the shouts of the boys engaged in their impromptu game caught his attention. The first school bell rang, breaking up the players into smaller groups who walked along talking, laughing, and patting each other on the back. Those boys sure did make it look easy and fun. But it was no fun for Tyler to watch from the out-side looking in. He thought he had more of a chance of becoming an astronaut than a basketball player.

Tyler settled into his chair on the second row of the classroom just as the second bell rang.

"Good morning, class," Miss Trimble began. "I have two announcements to make. First, basketball tryouts will be held toward the end of the month. It's an after-school co-ed team that the gym teacher is organizing. Everyone is encouraged to practice all month and participate. Second, in honor of Columbus Day on October 12, all fifth-grade students are required to write a report on the great explorer Christopher Columbus. Reports will be presented orally in front of the class on the last Friday of the month."

The teacher was still talking, but that was about all Tyler heard. She might as well have announced that October was "Laugh at the Loser" Month. Tyler couldn't think of any two *worse* things than trying out for a sport or giving an oral report. He would rather eat nothing but broccoli for a solid month!

Miss Trimble had assembled dozens of reference materials for the students to use in preparing their Columbus reports. They all looked the same to Tyler, who stood staring at them blankly.

"Here, try this one," called pretty Chloe Cooper, tossing him a book. Tyler looked just in time for *The Early Life of Christopher Columbus* to smack him in the face and fall to the classroom floor with a loud *THUD*.

"Hey, why don't you try out for offense? You're *so good* at catching passes!" taunted Charlie Chambers, the school bully. The class erupted in laughter.

Tyler could feel the heat spreading from his ears to his cheeks, turning them red. He quickly grabbed the book from the floor and moved to his safe haven between the dusty old bookshelf and the back corner of the classroom.

CHAPTER TWO

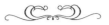

Columbus at Eleven

Tyler moved his fingers all around the cover of *The Early Life of Christopher Columbus*. He opened the book and tried hard to read, but the words all seemed to run together; none of them stayed in his head. He squinted and tried harder to concentrate on the book in his hands. He read to himself, "Columbus was born somewhere between August 25 and October 31, 1451, in the seaport city of Genoa, Italy, to a master weaver named Domenico Columbus and his wife, Susanna, a wealthy weaver's daughter."

Tyler thought back to his first brief journey through Miss Trimble's trapdoor and how he had seen Columbus in 1492. But what was the great explorer like when he was a boy? Adding eleven years to 1451, Tyler came up with the year 1462. That would make Columbus eleven years old, just like Tyler and many of his classmates. The fifth grader's feet reached for the baseboards, longing for knowledge and an escape from the humiliation he felt.

"1462...1462...1462," he chanted and attempted the trapdoor dance that had worked several times before. Left foot tap...right foot tap...left foot tap...right stomp!

Tyler felt the relief of the familiar falling sensation. He landed in the green beanbag chair so thoughtfully placed beneath the trapdoor by his wise stray dog friend, Barnabas Bailey.

"I see you have been doing some reading," noted Barney.

Tyler looked down at the book, still in his hands. "Yes, I have to do a report on Columbus. An *oral* report!"

"And so you shall. An outstanding one at that, I might add," encouraged Barney, motioning with his paw for Tyler to follow along.

"Well, I'll do my best," Tyler said, trying to sound confident as he walked behind the brown furry tail toward the wall of bookshelves. He reached for the neat little row of titles and used his sleeve to wipe a bit of dust off the first book, *The Perseverance of Christopher Columbus*. After setting his schoolbook on the shelf, Tyler picked up the old book. He thumbed through the pages as he turned to walk with Barney.

"You know, Tyler, Columbus was a lot like you when he was your age. He did not want to be a weaver like his father and grandfather. He had other goals for himself, and perseverance."

"What's that mean?"

"It means he kept trying and never gave up, just like you are learning to do," explained the dog.

Just then, Tyler looked up to see a boy a little smaller than himself crouched on the tide line of a beach near his home on the Portuguese island of Madeira. The sun was high overhead, warming the tan sand as the

7

waves came in slowly. The tiny boy was not distracted by the heat or the squawking birds.

"Boy, I thought I was scrawny for eleven!" commented Tyler.

"Children five hundred years ago did not have the variety of nutritious foods we have today to help us grow," explained the wise guide dog.

Young Columbus had red hair, blue eyes, and freckles. He had a book by Marco Polo tucked under his arm, and he was kneeling over some items washed up on the beach.

Barney continued, "Reading about Marco Polo's adventures made Chris very curious. He wanted to explore too! And when he found strange plants and carved wood that no one had ever seen before, he knew the ocean must have washed them up from some unknown land...a land he couldn't wait to find for himself!"

CHAPTER THREE

COLUMBUS BLUES

"Is that why Columbus decided to become a cabin boy on a ship when he was fourteen?" Tyler asked, pointing to a page in his book.

"Exactly," replied Barney with a pleased expression on his furry face. "And why he soon began sailing all over the known world."

As they walked farther down the beach, Tyler saw something burning in the ocean waters. It was a ship! Tyler spotted a grown man clinging desperately to a piece of wood in the waters near the sinking vessel. "Is that Columbus?" he asked, shocked.

"I'm afraid so," answered Barney. "The year is now 1476, and Columbus is twenty-five. His ship was sailing to England but was attacked by French pirates and sank. Our famous explorer of course survives and recovers in Lagos, Portugal. By 1477, he and his brother Bartholomew were running a map shop in the ocean town of Lisbon, Portugal. He married Dona Felipa Moniz de Perestrello in 1479 and had a son named Diego in 1480."

Tyler stopped to dump the sand out of his sneakers as he and Barnabas Bailey walked beyond the beach onto what Barney explained were the streets of Spain. These roads were not paved and smooth like the ones Tyler was used to seeing at home. The boy and dog could not help but stir up the dirt as they walked along the bumpy way. There Tyler spied Columbus. He was a few years older, and he was obviously discouraged. He walked along looking down with his shoulders hunched, just as Tyler did when he felt like giving up.

"Why is he so down? I thought you said he had persee, persaaa..." stuttered Tyler.

"Perseverance, yes. But everyone feels disheartened sometimes when things go wrong, even great explorers. You need to do some studying and find out what had our explorer friend feeling so low."

The words had barely left the dog guide's mouth when Tyler was back in his area of the classroom. No one seemed to have missed him. He began reading his reference books with new enthusiasm. He made a list of the things that had happened to Columbus between 1484 and 1488:

1. He asked King John II of Portugal to give him money for ships to explore, but the king said NO.
2. He asked the Royal Portuguese Commission for money for ships, but they said NO.
3. His wife Felipa died.
4. He asked King Ferdinand and Queen Isabella of Spain for money for ships,

but they were too busy fighting a war and said NO.

5. He asked King Charles VIII of France and King Henry VII of England for money for ships, but they both said NO.

No wonder Columbus looked so discouraged! He really had to have perseverance to keep trying even after so many sad things happened. None of the royalty at the time wanted to help him discover what was beyond the known world traveling west across the Atlantic Ocean, which back then was called the Ocean Sea.

CHAPTER FOUR

RECESS PRACTICE

Feeling a little braver after his adventures with Barney and young Columbus, Tyler grabbed a basketball from the recess bucket and headed for a remote area of the playground. No one ever used this goal, so perhaps no one would notice him. He tried to dribble the ball, but it hit his foot and went rolling instead. He tried to make a shot, but it didn't come close. Charlie and a few other boys started walking his direction. He held the ball still and wished he could be invisible.

"I don't think a month is enough time for you to practice. You need more like a *year*," taunted Charlie. The other boys laughed and agreed.

"Nah, keep at it, Tyler. You'll get the hang of it," came a voice in the back.

It was Dillon Davis, the most popular boy in school!

Out of the corner of his eye, Tyler could make out the tall, slim frame of Mr. Jenkins, the school janitor, as he carried out some trash to the dumpster beside the basketball court. "He's right, kiddo. If old Chris Columbus had to work at his game, I imagine so do you," he reasoned with a wink and a smile. The easy, slow voice of the kind custodian had a calming effect on the boy's shaky hands.

The schoolyard stray sat at the edge of the basketball court. Mr. Jenkins knelt down and gave him a gentle pat on the head before leaving the playground. Barney sat straight up, intent on watching Tyler practice.

"Toss it here," called Chloe.

Tyler's hands were sweaty and froze on the ball for a moment. Then he gave it his best shot. Her pretty blond hair twirled around her face as she caught it, aimed for the basket, and SWOOSH. Chloe made a perfect shot.

"Don't think I could have done that with a library book," she giggled. It was the perfect ending to an otherwise embarrassing recess.

CHAPTER FIVE

THE BRAVE BELIEVERS

Tyler walked a little taller as he settled back into his familiar work area in Miss Trimble's classroom. Miss Trimble had given the class an extra study period to work on their Columbus research. Tyler had lots of good notes for his report all the way up to the year 1492. He remembered visiting that year before through the trapdoor, but was excited to learn more. "1492...1492...1492," he muttered a little louder than he should have.

"Miss Trimble, will you ask Tyler to BE QUIET? I'm *trying* to work on my report," demanded Madison Martinez. Nervously, Tyler tapped left, right, left, and right stomped as fast as he could.

BAM! He landed hard on the cold cement of the basement floor. Before he could ask why, he discovered the answer. A few feet away was the green beanbag chair. This time it had more than brown and white dog hairs on it. It had a brown and white *dog*. Mr. Barnabas Bailey, the wise old mutt, was curled up sound asleep looking very common. After retrieving the Columbus book off the bookshelf, Tyler reached down to pet Barney like he had done so many times before in the schoolyard before he learned how very uncommon the dog really was. The kind brown eyes opened slowly. "Oh, do pardon me, I had no thought that you would be inclined to return so soon," apologized Barney.

"It's just that I want to know what happened to Columbus after all those bad things," explained Tyler.

"Let's find out," yawned Barney, stretching and rising to walk upright on his hindquarters alongside the boy. "Spain had won the war by 1492, but it, like many other European countries, was still very interested in finding another route to the East Indies, or what we now know as China, India, Japan, and the surrounding islands, to look for spices and gold."

"So King Ferdinand and Queen Isabella decided to help Columbus?" asked Tyler.

"Well, not right away," explained Barney. "The Spanish king was not convinced. The queen was more inclined, but couldn't make up her mind. At first she said no. Then a powerful official of the Spanish court named Luis de Santangel advised her to support Columbus. Our explorer friend was four miles out of town by the time the queen's courier gave him the good news.

"But there was more convincing yet to be done. Columbus needed a crew, but the sailors were terrified of what they called the Sea of Darkness. They had heard stories of sea monsters swallowing up ships or ships sailing off the edge of the world. No one had *ever* sailed that far out into the Ocean Sea."

"Didn't anyone believe in Columbus's theory that he could reach the East Indies by sailing west?" asked Tyler.

"Not many. The Royal Decree of April 30, 1492, even gave any criminals their freedom if they would sail with Columbus, but only four men took the deal and signed up. It wasn't until a respected shipper named Martin Alonzo Pinzón decided to sail with Columbus that other sailors took notice and followed his lead," the studious dog said.

Tyler thought that Pinzón and the brave criminals were kind of like Dillon and Chloe and Mr. Jenkins. Columbus had a few people who believed in him, and now so did Tyler.

CHAPTER SIX

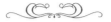

THE FAMOUS VOYAGE

Tyler was growing weary from the long walk down the dusty streets of the Spanish town of Palos de la Frontera toward the docks with Barney. Then he saw *them*. The three ships! Three ancient wooden ships lined up along the shore of the River Tinto. His eyes grew wide. This must be the Niña; it was the smallest of the three. Next was the Pinta, and finally the largest, the Santa Maria! All of the ships were less than thirty feet wide and no longer than a tennis court. The Pinta and the Niña were about seventy to eighty feet long.

"Quickly, board with me, young Tyler," directed the brown and white mongrel as he scurried onto the Santa Maria. "We shall sail on the ship under Captain Columbus and his forty crewmen." Barney explained that Martin Alonzo Pinzón was the captain of the Pinta and its twenty-six men while Pinzón's brother headed up the Niña's twenty-four men.

Tyler was excited to be on the Santa María with Columbus. It was definitely the biggest of the three, but it looked much smaller in person than Tyler had imagined. No wonder the men on board were nervous. Tyler would have never stayed on the ship without Barney and the knowledge that they would arrive safely in the New World. How brave the shipmates must have been to sail where no one had gone before!

Barnabas Bailey pulled out a calendar that had been folded up in the back of the old book and handed it to Tyler. Then the dog curled up on the ship's wooden deck. Sitting cross-legged beside his wiry-haired friend, Tyler noted the date Barney had circled: August 3, 1492. This was the day Columbus and his three ships set sail. The boy held on tight as the ship moved into the ocean waters toward the Canary Islands. The shore drifted out of sight, and soon there was nothing to be seen but the endless Ocean Sea.

The wind began to blow the pages of the antique book. "Count the pages blown, boy. That indicates how many days have passed. Record it on your calendar," explained the wise dog. Patiently, Tyler marked off three days on his calendar. It was yellowed with age and had crease marks from where it had been folded. After those three days, Barney pointed out where the mast of the Pinta had been damaged. The book's pages were mysteriously blowing past again. Nine pages blown; it took nine days to reach the Canary Islands to repair it. Tyler was weary already! He couldn't imagine if he had actually been a crewmember living through all those days at sea. He thought he would not have made a very good sailor. He listened to the others talk of their anticipation. Many were looking forward to finding gold, spices, and other riches in the East Indies. Others admitted to some apprehension over what dangers might lay ahead.

All ninety of the men prepared to leave the Canary Islands on September 6. Tyler was getting the hang of keeping track of time using his calendar and the magic of the book from the school basement, which seemed to move things in fast forward. The three determined ships sailed out into the unchartered Atlantic Ocean. The newly repaired Pinta proved to be the fastest of all. Tyler faithfully marked the days off on his calendar each time the winds of time blew the pages in his old book forward. Soon each day seemed to blur into the next. The swaying of the ship beneath him made Tyler forget what solid ground felt like. He even missed taking a bath! Tyler thought that he would never complain about school lunches again. He was incredibly tired of the same diet of hard biscuits, beans, and especially the oversalted meat and fish. Barney explained that salt was the only way of keeping foods fresh before refrigeration. Fresh water was limited, and the grown sailors sometimes drank wine. The boy and dog were invisible to the crew, but apparently not the few animals aboard. Barney tolerated the cats that roamed the ship freely to keep down the mice population, but he was not overly friendly.

Twice the men became fearful. The first time was when the Santa Maria became stuck in seaweed. The sailors feared they would be overtaken or be unable to move. Another time the wind calmed so much that the ships stood still. Even knowing the final outcome, Tyler was nervous. When the ships became mobile again, some of the sailors wanted to turn around. They were exhausted and fearful. But each time, Columbus, confident in his dream, would call out "*Adelante!*" which means "onward."

Tyler was sound asleep aboard the Santa Maria. It was two o'clock in the morning and very dark. His slumber was disturbed by a sailor on the Pinta named Rodrigo. He was shouting at the top of his lungs,

"*Tierra!*" or "land." Tyler looked down at his calendar in the moonlight. He circled the date: October 12, 1492. It had been seventy-one long days since leaving Spain.

CHAPTER SEVEN

EXPLORATION OF A NEW WORLD

Tyler remembered this island from his very first visit down Miss Trimble's trapdoor. It was San Salvador, also called Guanahani by the natives, in the Bahamas, 375 miles southeast of Florida. Columbus was claiming the island for Spain in the name of King Ferdinand and Queen Isabella. Tyler wondered what the native people living on the island must have thought. They were shy but curious, wearing very little clothing and peering out from behind trees to get a better look at the ships and sailors. Once they ventured out, they were friendly and gladly accepted the bells, glass beads, and red caps offered to them in trade. In return they gave balls of cotton and big colorful birds called parrots that Europeans had never seen. Tyler saw some of the native people cut their hands while inspecting the Spaniards' swords. He heard Columbus and the other sailors mumbling that the people would make good slaves because they knew nothing of weapons. That made Tyler very sad. Queen Isabella would not have liked that idea either!

Columbus thought he had landed in the East Indies, so he called the native Taíno people "Indians" by mistake. Tyler learned that he was not the only one who had trouble in math, especially in estimation. The great explorer had made another error. Columbus estimated that the distance between Western Europe and Asia across the ocean was roughly 2,400 miles. In reality it is about 10,000 miles! Of course, like other people of that time, Columbus had no idea that the two great continents of North and South America lie between Europe and Asia.

Eager to find more of the gold they had seen in the noses of the Taíno people, Columbus and his crew searched other islands in the Caribbean. They explored Cuba and La Española, also called Hispañola. They were disappointed to find very little of the precious metal and decided to return to Spain toward the end of December.

Tyler settled back in on the Santa Maria with all the fascinating treasures Columbus had collected to impress the Spanish royalty. The boy nested in between cotton, lizard skins, interesting new plants and shells, a little gold, and the hugest rats he had ever seen. Tyler loved the beautiful parrots, and Barney seemed to enjoy the company of a strange new breed of dog that was unable to bark. Tyler wondered how the six young Taíno men aboard must have felt. He thought they probably missed their family and friends back in the Bahamas, just like Tyler was beginning to miss his. He thought if they had a choice, they would not have gone to Spain.

Tyler's tummy was full, and he was becoming sleepy after a good meal. He had sampled new and delicious island food such as corn, potatoes, peanuts, papayas, avocadoes, and pineapples. What a wonderful change from the hard biscuits and salty meats on the trip from Spain! At home Tyler would have been chilly around Christmas time, but the tropical island air was warm and relaxing. Both excited about all he had seen and eager to return to Europe, Tyler drifted off in peaceful slumber.

His dreams were disturbed by the shouting of the crewmen and the sensation of cold saltwater on his shoes and pants. The Santa Maria had wrecked! Chief Guacanagari ordered his people to assist, but it was no use. Columbus's ship could not be saved.

The Pinta and Niña could not hold all ninety sailors. Determined to persevere, however, Columbus used the wood from the Santa Maria to build a fort on La Española, or what is now modern Haiti, for the thirty-nine men who had to be left behind. The fort was named La Navidad, which means "Christmas" in Spanish.

A dangerous journey from the Bahamas back to Europe lay ahead of Columbus and his crew in the two remaining ships. The Niña and Pinta arrived back on Spanish soil on March 15, 1493, having been away for thirty-two weeks.

CHAPTER EIGHT

SIGN HERE

"All right, class, let's line up for PE," announced Miss Trimble. "I would really like to see everyone sign up to try out for basketball." She sure made it sound simple.

Tyler thought about it all the way down the hallway. Compared to all the hardships Columbus had to endure, basketball tryouts shouldn't seem too scary. But then again, Columbus hadn't been in the fifth grade with kids like Charlie either.

Ignoring the sharp shove on his left shoulder from Charlie, Tyler got in line for the sign-up sheet in the gym. He stared straight ahead at Chloe's long, pretty, blond hair in front of him. It was so close he could smell her sweet shampoo. It was a fantastic distraction from the mumbles and giggles coming from Charlie and the other boys behind him.

Sooner than he had expected, he was staring Chloe in the face. He stood there motionless until he finally noticed her outstretched hand holding a black marker.

"Here ya go, Tyler. You *are* signing up, aren't you?" came the cheery, high-pitched voice. Chloe and Miss Trimble were apparently on the same page with how easy this should be. Maybe if you are pretty and smell nice, everything *is* easy. Tyler didn't think he qualified in the looks or aroma department. But with his hand shaking a little, he signed TYLER THOMPSON in his neatest penmanship, right under Chloe's big, loopy, girly writing.

He spent the rest of gym class in front of the basket, missing almost every shot. He imagined he was Columbus, and each shot was a request for funding for ships. Dribble, dribble, shoot. Miss. King John II of Portugal says NO. Shoot again. Miss. King Charles VIII of Spain Says NO. Dribble, shoot, and miss again. King Henry VII of England says NO. Shoot again. Miss by a long shot. King Ferdinand and Queen Isabella of Spain say NO. Focus the aim, dribble three times, and shoot again. This one goes in! The king and queen of Spain reconsider and give him the ships. Success!

Tyler liked game he was playing in his head, so he kept at it. Dribble, dribble, shoot. A miss...he has trouble finding sailors. Dribble, shoot, in it goes! Pinzón and some others sign on to sail. Dribble, dribble, shoot. Miss...seaweed stalls the ship. Miss again...lack of winds. Dribble, shoot, right in the basket! Land in sight! Tyler realized if you were going to make the basketball team or become Admiral of the Ocean Sea, you just had to keep trying.

CHAPTER NINE

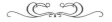

MORE VOYAGES

Tyler could barely walk down the hallway. There was a large pack of students crowded around a piece of paper on the gym door. He had been spending so much time on his Columbus report the past few days that he had almost forgotten that today was the day the gym teacher would post the roster for the basketball team! He had just been watching the students practice, so no one was really sure when the coach had made his decisions. Tyler could feel his heart beating hard in his chest as he searched for his name. His eyes anxiously scanned the list twice, but he didn't see it anywhere. Wait...there it was with an asterisk behind it, right under Dillon's name. Nobody else had an asterisk.

Before he could ask what that meant, Dillon answered the question for him.

"Hey, man, you're my alternate," explained Dillon. "That's pretty cool." Tyler didn't feel so cool, but he supposed it was better than a lot of kids who didn't make the team at all. He would get to play if Dillon couldn't.

The morning bell rang, and slowly the crowd dispersed and students headed to their classrooms.

"Today is the last day I am going to give you class time to work on your Columbus reports," said Miss Trimble. "We will devote this last Friday of October to presenting our reports orally. Let's use our time wisely since that's just two days away."

Tyler settled into his familiar work area between the dusty old bookshelf and the back corner of the room. He spread out all his notes. He had information about Columbus as a child, a young man, the first voyage to the New World, and back. He just needed to see what happened after that. Taking a deep breath, he stated the year of Columbus's return to Spain. "1493...1493...1493," he muttered while giving a left foot tap...right foot tap...left foot tap...right stomp!

"SHH!" snapped Madison, but Tyler had already disappeared down Miss Trimble's trapdoor. He landed with a thud on the green beanbag chair right alongside a sleeping Barnabas Bailey. Tyler wasn't sure who was more startled. The two friends were nose to muzzle, and Tyler thought he could smell dog biscuits on the mutt's breath as he gave out a yelp.

"Why, young Tyler, I did not know you would be joining me today," explained the wise dog.

"Yeah, I just need to finish my report, at least the stuff after Columbus returns to Spain."

"You don't need me for that, Tyler. You are doing fine on your own. You have learned much."

Tyler wanted to argue that he *did* still need Barney's help, but before he had time, he was back in the classroom. He was very confused as to why Barney had abandoned him. He stared at the books in front of him and tried to make sense of the words on the pages. If Barney believed he could do it, then he would give it his best effort.

He pushed hard with his pencil, putting what he read about the next voyages in his own words:

Columbus's second voyage was from September 25, 1493, to June 11, 1496. He took seventeen ships and fifteen hundred men to establish a Spanish colony. On November 28, 1493, he was ~~dissapointed~~ disappointed to find the fort of La Navidad burned and the men who had been left there dead. The native people had killed them in anger over the men's cruelty to them. Columbus discovered Dominica, Puerto Rico, and ~~Jamaka~~ Jamaica. He explored Cuba some more and named a city after Queen Isabella on La Española. He left his brother Bartholomew in charge of the city of Isabella.

Columbus's third voyage was from May 30, 1498, to late October or November 1500. He discovered Trinidad and South America before going back to La Española. The people there were mad at him and his brother, so Spain sent a judge named ~~Frans~~ Francisco de Bobadilla. The judge chained up Columbus and Bartholomew and sent them back to Spain. The queen took off the chains but let Bobadilla be in charge of the Spanish colonies from then on.

Columbus's fourth and last voyage was from early May 1502 to November 7, 1504. He ~~went to~~ explored Honduras and Panama. He shipwrecked in Jamaica and had to return to Spain.

CHAPTER TEN

COLUMBUS DAY

The knot in Tyler's stomach only grew as he walked into the classroom. It had been there since his alarm clock rang and he realized what today was. It was the final Friday of October, which in Miss Trimble's class meant ORAL REPORT DAY. Every footstep forward was an effort to fight the urge to flee. He felt like a small animal on one of those nature shows traipsing around an open field full of predators.

He clutched his report in his sweaty right hand. Thankfully, he had placed it in a transparent plastic folder or it would have been more than slightly soggy by now.

The rest of the class was talking and laughing before the morning bell. A paper airplane whizzed right by his nose, but nothing fazed the nervous fifth grader. He couldn't stand it much longer. He *had* to get this over with. He approached the teacher's desk. It seemed like he was hearing some one else's voice when he asked, "Miss Trimble, can I be first to give my oral report?"

"Of course you may, Tyler," she responded with a ready smile. "I'm so proud of your courage!"

Courage? Couldn't she hear his knees knocking or his heart pounding? He felt like the kindergarten kids down the hall could hear.

The first eight pages of Tyler's report seemed like a blur to him. He was reading the words on the page, but not really concentrating. He felt a little dizzy from the speed of his words. He turned the last page, took a deep breath, and continued:

During his last journey, when Columbus arrived at La Española on June 29, 1502, he again encountered trouble. He asked the governor to let his five ships enter because a terrible storm was coming. The governor just laughed at him and sent thirty ships full of treasures and men to sail back to Spain. Columbus was determined to survive and anchored his five ships. Twenty-nine of the governor's ships were destroyed, and five hundred men died. Columbus did not lose a ship or a single sailor!

He finally returned to Spain on November 7, 1504. Queen Isabella died in November of that same year, and King Ferdinand was not interested in sending Columbus on any more voyages. Columbus died on May 20, 1506, still not knowing he had discovered a whole new world. On October 12, 1892, on the four hundredth anniversary of the explorer's arrival on San Salvador Island, President Benjamin Harrison declared the first

Columbus Day. President Franklin Roosevelt made it a federal holiday in 1937.

Christopher Columbus was not the only one who believed that it was possible to reach the East by sailing west. We remember him because he had the perseverance to follow his dream.

Tyler finally looked up at the rest of the class and Miss Trimble. To his surprise, he seemed to have everyone's attention. The classroom was so quiet that the only sound was the ticking of the huge clock on the wall. Tyler had spoken for thirty whole minutes!

"I don't know what to say except that I am exceedingly impressed with your research and attention to detail, Tyler Thompson!" gushed Miss Trimble. "You must have utilized some amazing outside resources. You included information that wasn't in any of my books. Perhaps you can share those with us after class."

Tyler slid back into his chair, exhaling in relief. He opened up the clear plastic report cover to brush away several brown and white dog hairs.

CHAPTER ELEVEN

THE BIG GAME

Tyler yawned as he looked at the scoreboard. It seemed like he had been sitting on the bench for a week, and it wasn't even halftime yet. Not that he was complaining really. He tried to look busy by reading all the colorful banners urging the Freedom Elementary Eagles on to victory. The thick navy blue and red polyester jersey felt good against his skin. It was great to be a part of something, even if he was just an alternate. He passed the time by concentrating on the new sneakers his mom had bought him. He thought they looked a little *too* new without any scuffs on the bright white leather, but it would have hurt her feelings if he hadn't worn them.

A loud buzzer coming from the court caught his attention. It was halftime at last. His teammates followed the coach to the locker room in a rowdy herd, but Tyler lagged behind. He really didn't feel a part of the team, and he wasn't sure if he even wanted to be if it meant having to play in front of the whole school.

"Why so down in the mouth, son?" Tyler recognized the familiar soothing voice of Mr. Jenkins. He thought the kind school janitor looked a little out of place wearing a T-shirt instead of his usual campus uniform shirt with his name sewn on the left shoulder.

"I dunno...I want to play, but I'm scared. It's probably best that I'm just an alternate."

"You wear the same uniform as all the others. You're every bit as good. You have heart and perseverance, just like an old explorer friend of ours."

"Columbus!" the boy and Mr. Jenkins said in unison. The old man had a contagious smile that Tyler couldn't help returning.

Tyler made it to the locker room just as all the others were storming back onto the court. He *was* wearing the same uniform as everyone else, he thought, joining the team.

Tyler sat on the bench, now watching the ball a lot more closely than his shoes. The score was close, with neither team gaining much of a lead before the other caught up. He watched Dillon dribble toward the basket for what looked like a perfect lay-up, but he collided with another boy right before the buzzer sounded. The third quarter ended in a 28-28 tie and Dillon writhing in pain on the floor holding is knee.

"This is it, Tyler, you're up," called the coach as the nurse got some ice for the star player.

The terrified fifth grader ran out onto the court, hoping no one knew how scared he was. His eyes met his opponent as they prepared for the tip-off. Up jumped Tyler, but the other kid smacked the ball over his head. The next few minutes seemed like hours as he seemed to do nothing more than chase the ball around the court while others dribbled, passed, and shot. Finally, he felt the ball hit his chest hard as Charlie tossed it to him. He was close to the basket, so he shot. And missed! He felt like young Columbus after the shipwreck, hanging desperately to a piece of wood surrounded by the endless ocean.

"Loser!" Charlie shouted just as Chloe rebounded the ball. The scoreboard read 40-40.

She was surrounded by the bright green jerseys of the other team, and she was calling Tyler's name. He held his hands high as Chloe threw the ball to him with all her might. He had to jump to catch it. He held on tight and turned toward the basket. Time was running out.

"Tyler! Tyler! Tyler!" chanted the crowd. The homemade posters seem to be waving in slow motion across the gymnasium. "Go Eagles!" read one. "Freedom Elementary #1!" declared another. "You can do it Red and Blue!" said a third. He took a deep breath, aimed, and closed his eyes as the ball slid off his fingertips. The orange ball circled the rim, then sank right into the goal just before the final buzzer.

He had won the game for his team!

Tyler got lost in the excitement of all the high fives and pats on the back from everyone, even Charlie. Over the cheering of the crowd, he heard barking. There was Barnabas Bailey under the goal, congratulating him in his own way. Tyler had never been more proud of himself and the perseverance he had learned from Christopher Columbus.

SUGGESTED READING

For Younger Readers

- *Christopher Columbus: A Great Explorer (A Rookie Biography)* by Carol Greene
- *Christopher Columbus (A Step into Reading Level 2 Book)* by Stephen Krensky
- *Christopher Columbus...Who Sailed On!* by Dorothy Fay Richards
- *Columbus Day* by Vicki Liestman
- *Follow the Dream: The Story of Christopher Columbus* by Peter Sis
- *In 1492* by Jean Marzollo
- *Meet Christopher Columbus* by James T. de Kay
- *A Picture Book of Christopher Columbus* by David A. Adler

For Advanced Readers or for Teacher Reference

- *Christopher Columbus: Great Explorer* by David A. Adler

- *Christopher Columbus: Voyager to the Unknown* by Nancy Smiler Levinson

- *Discovering Christopher Columbus: How History is Invented* by Kathy Pelta

- *If You Were There in 1492* by Barbara Brenner

- *The Quest of Columbus* by Robert Meredith and E. Brooks Smith

- *The World's Great Explorers: Christopher Columbus* by Zachary Kent

THE SHIPS OF CHRISTOPHER COLUMBUS

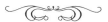

The First Voyage

All three ships less than 30 feet wide
Both smaller ships about 70–80 feet long

The Pinta

Fastest of the three ships
Captain Martin Alonzo Pinzón
26 crewmen
Caught in hurricane & sank in 1500

The Niña

Smallest of the three ships
Captain Vincente Yanez Pinzón
24 crewmen
Also in 2nd & 3rd voyages
Sold in 1499

The Santa Maria

Largest and slowest of the three ships
Captain Christopher Columbus
40 crewmen
Sank in December 1492
Wreckage used to build fort of La Navidad

The Second Voyage

17 ships
1,200–1,500 crewmen

The Third Voyage

6 ships
226 crewmen

The Fourth Voyage

4 ships
140 crewmen
Columbus's 13-year-old son Ferdinand joins
the crew

CHRISTOPHER COLUMBUS TIMELINE

- **1451**: Born between August 25 and October 31 in Genoa, Italy, to Domenico and Susanna Columbus

- **1476**: Becomes shipwrecked and moves to Portugal

- **1479**: Marries Dona Felipa Moniz de Perestrello

- **1480**: Has a son named Diego

- **1488**: Has a second son named Ferdinand

- **1492**: August 3: First voyage begins; sailed from Spain
  October 12: Lands on San Salvador Island

- **1493-1496**: Second voyage

- **1498-1500**: Third voyage

- **1500**: Arrested and sent back to Spain

1502: Fourth voyage begins

1503: Shipwrecked in Jamaica

1504: Rescued and returns to Spain

1506: May 20: Died at Valladolid, Spain

Europe

Portugal

Spain

ry Islands

Africa

Columbus's Voyages
1492 - 1504

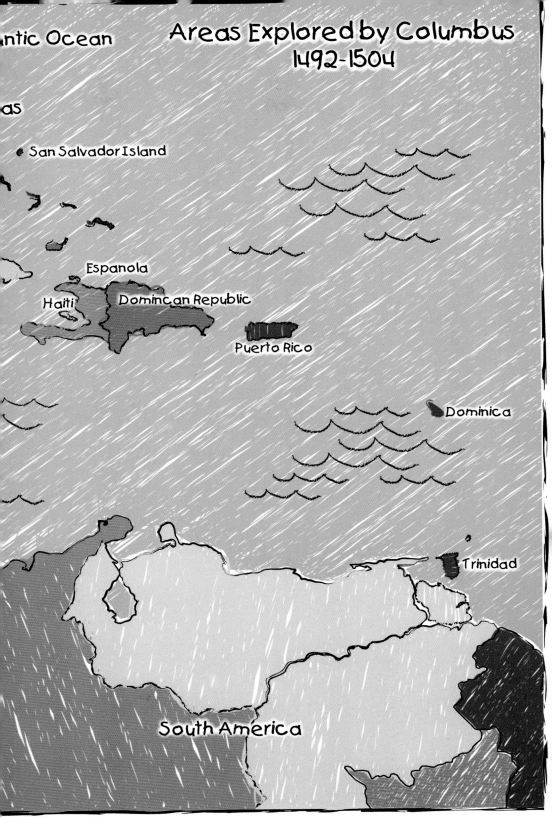